MODERATO
CANTABILE

by Marguerite Duras

translated by Richard Seaver

CALDER PUBLICATIONS · LONDON

First published in Great Britain in 1966 by
Calder & Boyars Limited and reprinted in 1987 by
John Calder (Publishers) Limited

This edition reprinted in Great Britain in 1997 by
Calder Publications Limited
179 Kings Cross Road, London WC1X 9BZ

Originally published in France in 1958 by
Les Editions de Minuit, Paris

ISBN 0 7145 0381 9

British Library Cataloguing in Publication Data
A catalogue record of this book is available from the British Library

Printed in Great Britain by Ebenezer Baylis & Son Ltd, Worcester.

TO G. J.

MODERATO
CANTABILE

"Will you please read what's written above the score?" the lady asked.

"Moderato cantabile," said the child.

The lady punctuated his reply by striking the keyboard with a pencil. The child remained motionless, his head turned towards his score.

"And what does moderato cantabile mean?"

"I don't know."

A woman, seated ten feet away, gave a sigh.

"Are you quite sure you don't know what moderato cantabile means?" the lady repeated.

The child did not reply. The lady stifled an exasperated groan, and again struck the keyboard with her pencil. The child remained unblinking. The lady turned.

"Madame Desbaresdes, you have a very stubborn little boy."

Anne Desbaresdes sighed again.

"You don't have to tell me," she said.

The child, motionless, his eyes lowered, was the only one to remember that dusk had just exploded. It made him shiver.

"I told you the last time, I told you the time before that, I've told you a hundred times, are you sure you don't know what it means?"

The child decided not to answer. The lady looked again at the object before her, her rage mounting.

"Here we go again," said Anne Desbaresdes under her breath.

"The trouble is," the lady went on, "the trouble is you don't want to say it."

Anne Desbaresdes also looked again at this child, from head to toe, but in a different way from the lady.

"You're going to say it this minute," the lady shouted.

The child showed no surprise. He still didn't reply. Then the lady struck the keyboard a third time, so hard that the pencil broke. Right next to the child's hands. His hands were round and milky, still scarcely formed. They were clenched and unmoving.

"He's a difficult child," Anne Desbaresdes offered timidly.

The child turned his head towards the voice, quickly towards his mother, to make sure of her existence, then resumed his pose as an object, facing the score. His hands remained clenched.

"I don't care whether he's difficult or not, Madame Desbaresdes," said the lady. "Difficult or not, he has to do as he's told, or suffer the consequences."

In the ensuing silence the sound of the sea came in through the open window. And with it the muffled noise of the town on this spring afternoon.

"For the last time. Are you sure you don't know what it means?"

A motorboat was framed in the open window. The child, facing his score, hardly moved—only his mother noticed it—as the motorboat passed through his blood. The low purr of the motor could be heard throughout the town. There were only a few pleasure craft. The whole sky was tinted pink by the last rays of the sun. Outside, on the docks, other children stopped and looked.

"Are you really sure, for the last time now, are you sure you don't know what it means?"

Again, the motorboat passed by.

The lady was taken aback by such stubbornness. Her anger abated, and she so despaired at being so unimportant to this child who, by a single gesture, she could have made to answer her, that she was suddenly aware of the sterility of her own existence.

"What a profession, what a profession," she lamented.

Anne Desbaresdes made no comment, but tilted her head slightly as if, perhaps, agreeing.

The motorboat had finally passed from the frame of the open window. The sound of the sea arose, boundless, in the child's silence.

"Moderato?"

The child opened his fist, moved it, and lightly scratched his calf. His gesture was unconstrained, and perhaps the lady admitted its innocence.

"I don't know," he said, after he had finished scratching himself.

The color of the sunset suddenly became so magnificent that it changed the gold of the child's hair.

"It's easy," the woman said a bit more calmly.

She blew her nose.

"What a child," Anne Desbaresdes said happily, "really, what a child! How in the world did I happen to have such an obstinate . . ."

The lady decided that such pride deserved no comment.

"It means," she said to the child, as though admitting defeat, "for the hundredth time, it means moderately and melodiously."

"Moderately and melodiously," the child said mechanically.

The lady turned around.

14

"Really. I mean *really*."

"Yes, it's terrible," Anne Desbaresdes said, laughing, "stubborn as a goat. It's terrible."

"Begin again," the lady said.

The child did not begin again.

"I said begin again."

The child still did not move. The sound of the sea again filled the silence of his stubbornness. The pink sky exploded in a final burst of color.

"I don't want to learn how to play the piano," the child said.

In the street downstairs a woman screamed, a long, drawn-out scream so shrill it overwhelmed the sound of the sea. Then it stopped abruptly.

"What was that?" the child shouted.

"Something happened," the lady said.

The sound of the sea moved in again. The pink sky began to fade.

"No," said Anne Desbaresdes, "it's nothing."

She got up and went to the piano.

"You're so nervous," the lady said, looking at both of them with a disapproving air.

Anne Desbaresdes took her child by the shoulders, shook him, and almost shouted:

"You've got to learn the piano, you've got to."

The child was also trembling, for the same reason, because he was afraid.

"I don't like the piano," he murmured.

15

Scattered shouts followed the first, confirming an already established fact, henceforth reassuring. So the lesson went on.

"You've got to," Anne Desbaresdes insisted.

The lady shook her head, disapproving such tenderness. Dusk began to sweep over the sea. And the sky slowly darkened, except for the red in the west, till that faded as well.

"Why?" the child asked.

"Because music, my love . . ."

The child took his time, trying to understand, did not understand, but admitted it.

"All right. But who screamed?"

"I'm waiting," said the lady.

He began to play. The music rose above the murmur of a crowd that was beginning to gather on the dock beneath the window.

"There now, there you are," Anne Desbaresdes said happily, "you see."

"When he wants to," the lady said.

The child finished the sonatina. The noise from the street grew more insistent, invading the room.

"What's going on?" the child asked again.

"Play it again," the lady replied. "And don't forget: moderato cantabile. Think of a lullaby."

"I never sing him songs," Anne Desbaresdes said. "Tonight he's going to ask me for one, and he'll ask me so sweetly I won't be able to refuse."

The lady didn't want to listen. The child began to play Diabelli's sonatina again.

"B flat," the lady said sharply, "you always forget."

The growing clamor of voices of both sexes rose from the dock. Everyone seemed to be saying the same thing, but it was impossible to distinguish the words. The sonatina went innocently along, but this time, in the middle of it, the lady could take no more.

"Stop."

The child stopped. The lady turned to Anne Desbaresdes.

"I'm sure something serious has happened."

They all went to the window. To their left, some twenty yards from the building, a crowd had already gathered on the dock in front of the café door. From the neighboring streets people were running up to join the crowd. Everyone was looking into the café.

"I'm afraid this part of town . . ." the lady said.

She turned and took the boy's arm. "Start again, one last time, where you left off."

"What's happened?"

"Your sonatina."

The child played. He played it at the same tempo as before, and as the end of the lesson approached he gave it the nuances she wanted, moderato cantabile.

"It upsets me when he does as he's told like that," Anne Desbaresdes said. "I guess I don't know what

11

I want. It's a cross I have to bear."

The child went on playing well.

"What a way to bring him up, Madame Desbaresdes," the lady said almost happily.

Then the child stopped.

"Why are you stopping?"

"I thought . . ."

He began playing the sonatina again. The noise of the crowd grew increasingly loud, becoming so powerful, even at that height, that it drowned out the music.

"Don't forget that B flat in the key," the lady said, "otherwise it would be perfect."

Once again the music crescendoed to its final chord. And the hour was up. The lady announced that the lesson was finished for today.

"You'll have plenty of trouble with that one, I don't mind telling you," she said.

"I already do. He worries me to death."

Anne Desbaresdes bowed her head, her eyes closed in the painful smile of endless childbirth. Below, a welter of shouts and orders proved the consummation of an unknown incident.

"Tomorrow we'll know it perfectly," the lady said.

The child ran to the window.

"Some cars are coming," he said.

The crowd blocked both sides of the café entrance, and was still growing, but the influx from the neighboring streets had lessened. Still, it was much larger than one might have suspected. The people moved aside and made a path for a black van to get through. Three men got out and went into the café.

"Police," someone said.

Anne Desbaresdes asked what had happened.

"Someone's been killed. A woman."

She left her child in front of Mademoiselle Giraud's door, joined the body of the crowd, and made her way forward till she reached the front row of silent people looking through the open windows. At the far end of the café, in the semi-darkness of the back room, a woman was lying motionless on the floor. A man was crouched over her, clutching her shoulders, and saying quietly:

"Darling. My darling."

He turned and looked at the crowd; they saw his eyes, which were expressionless, except for the stricken, indelible, inward look of his desire. The patronne stood calmly near the van and waited.

"I tried to call you three times."

"Poor woman," someone said.

"Why?" Anne Desbaresdes asked.

"No one knows."

In his delirium the man threw himself on the inert

body. An inspector took him by the arm and pulled him up. He did not resist. It seemed that all dignity had left him forever. He looked absently at the inspector. The inspector let go of him, took a notebook and pencil from his pocket, asked for the man's identity, and waited.

"It's no use. I won't say anything now," the man said.

The inspector didn't press the matter, and went over to join his colleagues who were questioning the patronne at the last table in the back room.

The man sat down beside the dead woman, stroked her hair and smiled at her. A young man with a camera around his neck dashed up to the café door and took a picture of the man sitting there smiling. By the glare of the flash bulb the crowd could see that the woman was still young, and that blood was coming from her mouth in thin trickles, and that there was blood on the man's face where he had kissed her. In the crowd, someone said:

"It's horrible," and turned away.

The man lay down again beside his wife's body, but only for a moment. Then, as if he were tired, he got up again.

"Don't let him get away," the patronne shouted.

But the man had only got up in order to find a better position, closer to the body. He lay there, seemingly resolute and calm, holding her tightly in his arms, his face pressed to hers, in the blood flowing from her mouth.

But the inspectors had finished taking the patronne's testimony and slowly, in single file, walked over to him, an identical air of utter boredom on their faces.

The child, sitting obediently on Mademoiselle Giraud's front steps, had almost forgotten. He was humming the Diabelli sonatina.

"It was nothing," Anne Desbaresdes said. "Now we must go home."

The child followed her. More policemen arrived—too late, for no reason. As they passed the café the man came out, flanked by the inspectors. The crowd parted silently to let him through.

"He's not the one who screamed," the child said. "He didn't scream."

"No, it wasn't he. Don't look."

"Why did she. . . ?"

"I don't know."

The man walked meekly to the van. Then, when he reached it, he shook off the inspectors, and, without a word, ran quickly back towards the café. But just as he got there the lights went out. He stopped dead, again followed the inspectors to the van, and got inside. Then, perhaps, he was crying, but it was already too dark to see anything but his trembling, bloodstained face. If he was crying, it was too dark to see his tears.

"Really," Anne Desbaresdes said as they reached the Boulevard de la Mer, "you might remember it once and for all. Moderato means moderately slow, and cantabile means melodiously. It's easy."

DAY ②
Saturday

It was the following day. At the other end of town the factory chimneys were still smoking, and it was already later than when they went to the port every Friday.

"Come along," Anne Desbaresdes said to her child.

They walked along the Boulevard de la Mer. Some people were already out for a stroll. There were even a few in swimming.

The child was used to taking a daily walk through town with his mother, so that she could take him anywhere. But once they had passed the first breakwater and reached the place where the tugboats were moored just below Mademoiselle Giraud's house, he became frightened.

"Why did we come here?"

"Why not?" said Anne Desbaresdes. "Today we're only going for a walk. Come along. Here or somewhere else."

The child gave in, and followed her blindly.

She went straight to the bar. A man was there alone, reading a newspaper.

"A glass of wine," she ordered.

Her voice trembled. The patronne looked surprised, then composed herself.

"And for the child?"

"Nothing."

"This is where the scream came from, I remember," the child said.

He went over to the sun in the doorway, took a step down, and disappeared onto the sidewalk.

"A nice day," the patronne said.

She saw that the woman was trembling, and she avoided looking at her.

"I was thirsty," Anne Desbaresdes said.

"The first warm days, that's the reason."

"In fact, I think I'll have another glass of wine."

From the persistent trembling of the hands gripping the glass, the patronne realized that it would take a while to get the explanation she wanted, but that, once the emotion had passed, it would come of its own accord.

It came faster than she had expected. Anne Desbaresdes drank the second glass of wine without pausing.

"I was just passing," she said.

"It's nice weather for a walk," the patronne said.

The man had stopped reading his paper.

"At this time yesterday I was at Mademoiselle Giraud's."

Her hands were steadier, and the expression on her face was almost normal.

"I recognize you."

"There was a murder," the man said.

Anne Desbaresdes told a lie.

"I see . . . I was just wondering."

"That's natural enough."

"Of course," said the patronne. "I had a regular procession of people in here this morning."

The child outside was hopping on one foot.

"Mademoiselle Giraud is teaching my little boy to play the piano."

The wine must have helped, for her voice had also become more steady. A smile of deliverance slowly appeared in her eyes.

"He looks like you," said the patronne.

"That's what they say." The smile broadened.

"The eyes."

"I don't know," said Anne Desbaresdes. "You see . . . since I was taking him for a walk, I thought I might as well come here today. So . . ."

"Yes, a murder."

Anne Desbaresdes lied again.

"Ah . . . I didn't know."

A tugboat eased away from the dock, and got under way with a hot, even clatter of its engines. The child stood still on the sidewalk while the tugboat was maneuvering, then turned to his mother.

"Where's it going?"

She said she didn't know. The child left again. She picked up the empty glass in front of her, realized her mistake, set it down on the counter, and waited, her eyes lowered. Then the man came over.

"May I?"

She was not surprised, which upset her all the more.

"It's just that I'm not used to drinking, Monsieur."

He ordered some wine, and took another step towards her.

"The scream was so loud it's really only natural for people to try and find out what happened. I would have found it difficult not to, you know."

She drank her wine, the third glass.

"All I know is that he shot her through the heart."

Two customers came in. They recognized this woman at the bar and were surprised.

"And I don't suppose you can tell me why?"

It was obvious that she was not used to drinking wine, and that at this hour of the day she was generally doing something quite different.

"I wish I could, but I'm not really sure of anything."

"Perhaps no one knows?"

"He knew. He's gone out of his mind, been locked up since yesterday evening. As for her, she's dead."

The child ran in from outside and snuggled against his mother with a movement of happy abandon. She stroked his hair absent-mindedly. The man watched her more closely.

"They loved each other," he said.

She started, almost imperceptibly.

"Well, now do you know what the scream was about?" asked the child.

She did not answer, but shook her head no. The child moved again towards the door, her eyes following him.

"He worked at the dockyard. I don't know about her."

She turned towards him, moved closer.

"Perhaps they had problems, what they call emotional problems."

The customers left. The patronne, who had overheard, came to the corner of the bar.

"And she was married," she said, "three children, and she drank. It makes you wonder."

"But maybe it was like I said?" suggested Anne Desbaresdes, after a pause.

The man did not acquiesce. She was embarrassed.

And then her hands began to shake again.

"I really don't know . . ." she said.

"No," the patronne said, "take it from me, and generally I'm not one to meddle in other people's affairs."

Three new customers came in. The patronne moved away.

"Still, I think it might have been what you said," the man smiled. "Yes, they must have had emotional problems. Maybe that's why he killed her. Who knows?"

"Yes. Who knows?"

Mechanically the hand reached for the glass. He made a sign to the patronne for some more wine. Anne Desbaresdes did not protest; on the contrary, she seemed to expect it.

"From the way he acted with her," she said softly, "as if it didn't matter to him any more whether she was alive or dead, do you think that it's possible for anyone to reach such a . . . state . . . except . . . through despair?"

The man hesitated, looked directly at her, and said sharply:

"I don't know."

He handed her her glass; she took it and drank. Then he brought her back to topics that were doubt- less more familiar.

"You often go for walks through town?"

30

She drank a little wine, a smile came back to her face like a mask, more pronounced than before. She was becoming slightly drunk.

"Yes, I take my child for a walk every day."

He glanced at the patronne, who was talking to the three customers. It was Saturday. People had plenty of time to kill.

"But in this town, small as it is, something happens every day, as you well know."

"I know, but no doubt on some days . . . something happens to shock you," she stammered. "Usually I go to the parks or the beach."

And all the time, because of her growing intoxication, she brought herself to look more directly at the man in front of her.

"You've been taking him on these walks for a long time?"

The eyes of this man, who was talking to her and watching her at the same time.

"I mean you've been going to the parks and the beach for a long time," he went on.

She felt uncomfortable. Her smile vanished into a pout, which left her face brutally exposed.

"I shouldn't have drunk so much wine."

A siren wailed, announcing the end of work for the Saturday shift. Immediately afterwards the radio started to blare unbearably.

"Already six o'clock," the patronne said.

31

She turned the radio down, and busied herself setting up lines of glasses on the counter. Anne Desbaresdes remained looking dumbly at the docks for a minute, as if she were unable to decide what to do with herself. Then, as the distant noise of approaching men was heard from the port, the man spoke to her again.

"I was saying that you've been taking your child for walks to the beach or the parks for a long time now."

"I've thought about it over and over again since yesterday evening," said Anne Desbaresdes, "ever since my child's piano lesson. I couldn't help coming here today, you know."

The first men came in. The child, his curiosity aroused, made his way through them, and went up to his mother, who pulled him against her with a mechanical movement of protection.

"You are Madame Desbaresdes. The wife of the manager of Import Export et des Fonderies de la Côte. You live on the Boulevard de la Mer."

Another siren sounded, more faintly than the first, at the other end of the docks. A tugboat arrived. The child pulled himself brusquely away and ran off.

"He's learning to play the piano," she said. "He's talented enough, but he doesn't apply himself, I must admit."

In order to make room for the men who kept coming into the café in large numbers, he moved closer and closer to her. The first customer left. Others were still arriving. Between them, as they came and went, one could see the sun setting on the sea, the flaming sky, and the child who, on the other side of the dock, was playing all alone those games whose secret could not be discerned at that distance. He was jumping over imaginary hurdles and seemed to be singing.

"I want so many things for the child all at once that I don't know how to go about it, where to start. And I make a mess of it. I must be getting back because it's late."

"I've often seen you. I never imagined that one day you would come here with your child."

The patronne turned the radio up a little for the latecomers who had just come in. Anne Desbaresdes turned towards the bar, made a wry face, accepted the noise, forgot it.

"If you only knew how much happiness you really want for them, as if it were possible. Perhaps it would be better if we were separated from each other once in a while. I can't seem to understand this child."

"You have a beautiful house at the end of the Boulevard de la Mer. A big walled garden."

She looked at him quizzically, then came back to reality.

"But I get a lot of pleasure from these piano lessons," she said.

The child, trailed by twilight, came back towards them. He stayed there looking at the people, the customers. The man made a sign to Anne Desbaresdes to look outside. He smiled at her.

"Look," he said, "the days are getting longer and longer ..."

Anne Desbaresdes looked, adjusted her coat, carefully, slowly.

"Do you work here in town, Monsieur?"

"Yes, in town. If you came back here, I'd try to find out some more and tell you."

She lowered her eyes, remembered, and went pale.

"Blood on her mouth," she said, "and he was kissing her, kissing her." She went on: "Did you really believe what you said?"

"I said nothing."

The sun was now so low in the sky that it shone on the man's face. His body, leaning lightly against the bar, had been bathed in it for some time.

"Since you saw what happened, it wasn't possible to stop it, was it? It was almost inevitable?"

"I said nothing," the man repeated. "But I think he aimed at her heart, just as she asked him to."

Anne Desbaresdes sighed. A soft, almost erotic sigh.

"It's strange, I don't feel like going home," she said. Suddenly he took his glass, emptied it, made no answer, looked away from her.

34

"I must have drunk too much," she said. "That must be it."

"Yes, that must be it," the man said.

The café was nearly empty. Not many people were coming in now. The patronne watched them out of the corner of her eye while she washed glasses, intrigued to see them staying so late. The child, back at the door, gazed at the now silent docks. Standing before the man, her back to the port, Anne Desbaresdes said nothing for a long time. He seemed not to notice her presence.

"It would have been impossible for me not to come back," she said finally.

"And I came back too for the same reason as you."

"She's often out for a walk," the patronne said, "with her little boy. Every day in good weather."

"The piano lessons?"

"Once a week, on Fridays. Yesterday. This trouble actually gave her a reason for coming out today."

The man jingled the money in his pocket. He looked at the docks in front of him. The patronne did not press the matter further.

Past the breakwater the Boulevard de la Mer stretched out, perfectly straight to the edge of town.

"Lift your head," Anne Desbaresdes said. "Look at me."

The child, who was used to her ways, obeyed.

"Sometimes I think I must have invented you—that you don't really exist, you know."

The child lifted his head and yawned. His mouth was flooded with the last rays of the setting sun. Every time she looked at this child, Anne Desbaresdes was just as astonished as the first time she had seen him. But this evening her astonishment was greater than ever.

THREE

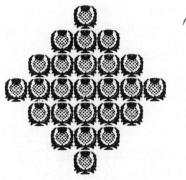

Tuesday

The child pushed the railing, his little school satchel bouncing up and down on his back, then he stopped at the entrance to the garden. He looked at the grass around him, tiptoed slowly, on the lookout, you never know, for the birds that he would have frightened away ahead of him. Just then a bird flew away. He watched it for a time, till it landed in a tree in the garden next door, then continued on his way till he was beneath a certain window behind a beech tree. He looked up. Every day at this time there was a smile for him at this window. The smile was there.

"Come on," shouted Anne Desbaresdes, "let's go for a walk."

"By the seashore?"

"By the seashore, everywhere. Come on."

Again they walked along the Boulevard de la Mer towards the breakwater. The child was quick to understand, and was not overly surprised.

"It's such a long way," he complained—then he resigned himself, and hummed a tune.

It was still early when they passed the first dock. The southern horizon was darkened by black streaks, ocher clouds spewed skyward by the foundries.

It was early, the café was empty, except for the man at the far end of the bar. As soon as she went in, the patronne got up and came over to Anne Desbaresdes. The man did not move.

"What'll it be?"

"I'd like a glass of wine."

She drank it as soon as it was served. She was trembling more than she had three days ago.

"I suppose you're surprised to see me again."

"Oh, in this business . . ." the patronne said.

She glanced surreptitiously at the man—he had also grown pale—sat down, then shifting her position, turned, and with a quick movement switched on the radio. The child left his mother and went out on the sidewalk.

"As I said, my little boy is taking piano lessons from Mademoiselle Giraud. You probably know her."

"Yes, I know her. For more than a year I've been seeing you go by, once a week, on Friday, right?"

"Yes, Friday. I'd like another glass of wine."

The child had found a friend. They stood motionless at the end of the dock watching the sand being unloaded from a barge. Anne Desbaresdes drank half of her second glass of wine. Her hands were a little steadier.

"He's a child who's always alone," she said, looking towards the end of the dock.

The patronne picked up her red sweater, and didn't answer. Another tugboat, loaded to the gunwales, entered the port. The child shouted something unintelligible. The man came over to Anne Desbaresdes.

"Won't you sit down?" he said.

She followed him without a word. As she knitted, the patronne followed the tugboat's every maneuver. It was obvious that in her opinion things were taking an unfortunate turn.

"Here."

He pointed out a table. She sat down across from him.

"Thank you," she murmured.

The room had a cool, dark air of early summer.

"I came back, you see."

Outside, not far away, a child whistled. She started.

"I'd like you to have another glass of wine," the man said, his eyes on the door.

He ordered the wine. The patronne silently obliged, no doubt already past worrying about the strangeness of their ways. Anne Desbaresdes sat back in her chair, momentarily relaxed, unafraid.

"It's been three days now," the man said.

She made an effort to sit up, and again drank her wine.

"It's good," she said quietly.

Her hands were steady now. She sat up straighter and leaned slightly forward towards the man, who was looking at her.

"I meant to ask you, you're not working today?"

"No, I need some free time for the moment."

Her smile was timidly hypocritical.

"Time to do nothing?"

"That's right, nothing."

The patronne was stationed at her post behind her cash register. Anne Desbaresdes spoke in an undertone.

"It's difficult for a woman to find an excuse to go into a café, but I told myself that I could surely think of something, like wanting a glass of wine, being thirsty . . ."

"I tried to find out something more. But I couldn't."

Anne Desbaresdes made an effort to remember again.

"It was a long, high-pitched scream, that stopped when it was at its loudest," she said.

"She was dying," the man said. "The scream must have stopped when she could no longer see him."

A customer came in, scarcely noticed them, and leaned on the bar.

"I think I must have screamed something like that once, yes, when I had the child."

"They met by chance in a café, perhaps even here, they both used to come here. And they began to talk to each other about this and that. But I don't know. Was it very painful when you had your child?"

"I screamed . . . You have no idea."

She smiled as she remembered, leaned back in her chair, suddenly completely free of her fear. He moved closer and said dryly:

"Talk to me."

She tried to find something to say.

"I live in the last house on the Boulevard de la Mer, the last one as you leave town. Just before the dunes."

"The magnolia tree in the left-hand corner of the garden is in bloom."

"Yes, there are so many flowers at this time of year that you can dream about them and be ill all the next day because of them. You shut your window, it's unbearable."

"It was in that house that you were married, some ten years ago?"

"Yes. My room is on the second floor, to the left, overlooking the sea. You told me last time that he had killed her because she had asked him to, to please her in fact?"

He waited before answering her, at last able to see the outline of her shoulders.

"If you shut your window at this time of year," he said, "you must be too hot to sleep."

Anne Desbaresdes became more serious than his remark seemed to call for.

"The scent of the magnolias is overpowering, you know."

"I know."

He raised his eyes from the line of her shoulders and looked away.

"Isn't there a long hallway on the second floor, a very long hallway into which your and everyone else's room opens, so that you're together and separated at the same time?"

"There's a hallway," Anne Desbaresdes said, "just as you say. But please tell me, how did she come to realize that that was what she wanted from him, how did she know so clearly what she wanted him to do?"

His eyes returned to hers, and he stared at her wearily.

"I imagine that one day," he said, "one morning at dawn she suddenly knew what she wanted him to do. Everything became so clear for her that she told him what she wanted. I don't think there's any explanation for that sort of discovery."

44

Outside the children were playing quietly. The second tug had reached the dock. In the silence after its motors had stopped, the patronne pointedly rattled some objects under the bar, reminding them that it was getting late.

"You were saying that it's necessary to go through this hallway to get to your room?"

"Yes, through the hallway."

The child ran in and laid his head on his mother's shoulder. She paid no attention to him.

"Oh, I'm having a lot of fun," he said, and raced out again.

"I forgot to tell you how much I wish he were already grown up," Anne Desbaresdes said.

He poured her some wine, handed her her glass, and she immediately drank it.

"You know," he said, "I suspect that he would have done it of his own accord one day, even without her asking. That she wasn't the only one to discover what she wanted from him."

She returned from her daydreams to her insistent, methodical questions.

"I'd like you to tell me about the very beginning, how they began to talk to each other. It was in a café, you said . . ."

The two children were running in circles, still playing at the end of the dock.

"We don't have much time," he said. "The factories close in a quarter of an hour. Yes, I'm almost sure it was in a café that they began to talk to each other, although it might have been somewhere else. Maybe they talked about the political situation, or the chances of war, or maybe something totally different from anything we can imagine, about everything and nothing. Perhaps we could drink one more glass of wine before you go back to the Boulevard de la Mer."

The patronne served them, still without a word, perhaps a trifle hastily. They paid no attention to her.

"At the end of this long hallway"—Anne Desbaresdes chose her words carefully—"there's a large bay window overlooking the boulevard. The wind lashes it like a whip. Last year, during a storm, the windows were smashed. It was at night."

She leaned back in her chair and laughed.

"To think that it happened here in this town . . . Really, it's hard to believe."

"Yes, it's a small town. Hardly enough people for the three factories."

The wall at the far end of the room was lighted by the setting sun. In the middle their two shadows were fused in black.

"And so they talked," said Anne Desbaresdes, "they talked for a long time, a very long time, before it happened."

"Yes, I think they must have spent a lot of time together to reach that stage. Talk to me."

"I don't know what else to say," she admitted.

He gave her an encouraging smile.

"What difference does it make?"

She began again, very slowly, with obvious effort and concentration.

"It seems to me that this house we were talking about was built somewhat arbitrarily, if you see what I mean, but nevertheless in such a way that it's convenient for everybody."

"On the ground floor there are rooms where receptions are given every year at the end of May for the people who work in the foundries."

The siren blasted unmercifully. The patronne got up, put her red sweater away, and rinsed the glasses that squeaked under the cold water

"You were wearing a black dress with a very low neck. You were looking at us pleasantly, indifferently. It was hot."

This did not surprise her, and she cheated.

"It's an exceptionally lovely spring," Anne Desbaresdes said, "everybody's talking about it. You think it was she who first brought it up, who first dared mention it, and that then they talked about it together as they talked about other things?"

"I don't know any more about it than you do. Maybe they only talked about it once, maybe every day. How will we ever know? But somehow they both reached exactly the same stage three days ago, where they no longer knew what they were doing."

He lifted his hand, let it fall close to hers on the table, and left it there. For the first time she noticed these two hands side by side.

"I've drunk too much wine again," she complained.

"Sometimes there's a light on till late at night in the hallway you mentioned."

"Sometimes I can't fall asleep."

"Why do you also keep the hall light on and not just a light in your room?"

"A habit of mine. I really don't know."

"Nothing happens there, nothing at night."

"Yes, behind one of the doors my child is sleeping."

She brought her arms back towards the table and, as if she were cold, pulled her coat around her shoulders.

"Perhaps I ought to be getting back. See how late it is."

He raised his hand as if asking her to stay. She stayed.

"The first thing in the morning, you go and look out of the big bay window."

"In summer the workers at the dockyards begin passing about six o'clock. In the winter most of them take the bus because of the wind and cold. It only lasts a quarter of an hour."

"At night, no one ever goes by—ever?"

"Yes, sometimes a bicycle, one wonders where it

came from. Is it the grief of having killed her, of her being dead, that drove him mad, or something else from his past added to that grief, something no one knows about?"

"I suspect there was indeed something else, something we don't know about yet."

She straightened up, slowly, as if she were being raised, and adjusted her coat again. He didn't help her. She still sat facing him, saying nothing. The first men came in, were surprised, gave the patronne a questioning look. The patronne gave a barely perceptible shrug, indicating that she herself didn't much understand what was going on.

"Perhaps you won't come back again."

When he in turn stood up, Anne Desbaresdes must have noticed that he was still young, that the setting sun was reflected in his eyes as clearly as in a child's. She looked past his gaze into his blue eyes.

"I hadn't thought that I might never come back here."

He detained her one last time.

"You often watch those men on their way to the dockyards, especially in summer, and at night, when you have trouble sleeping, they come back to you."

"When I wake up early enough," Anne Desbaresdes admitted, "I watch them. And you're right, sometimes at night the memory of some of them comes back to me."

As they left, some other workers emerged onto the docks. They were probably workers from the Fonderies de la Côte, which was farther from town than the dockyards. It was lighter out than it had been three days before. There were some seagulls in the sky, which was now blue again.

"I had fun playing," the child said.

She let him talk about his games till they had passed the first breakwater, from which the Boulevard de la Mer stretched straight as far as the dunes, where it ended.

The child grew impatient.

"What's the matter?"

As twilight fell the wind began to rise. She was cold.

"I don't know. I'm cold."

The child took his mother's hand, opened it and clasped it implacably, resolutely in his. She was overwhelmed by the gesture, and almost shouted:

"Oh, my love!"

"But you're going again."

"I expect so."

They passed some people on their way home who were carrying folding chairs. The wind lashed them in the face.

"What are you going to buy me?"

"A red motorboat. Would you like that?"

The child weighed the thought in silence, then sighed happily.

"Yes, a big red motorboat. How did you think of it?"

She took him by the shoulders, and held him as he tried to squirm loose to run on ahead.

"You're growing up, oh, you're getting so big, and I think it's wonderful."

Wednesday
Thursday

Music

Again the next day Anne Desbaresdes took her child to the port. The lovely weather persisted, only a little cooler than the day before. The sky was increasingly clear, overcast only at rare intervals. The whole town was talking about the unseasonably good weather. Some voiced the fear that it would end the next day, it had already lasted so unusually long. Others felt sure that the brisk wind sweeping the town would keep the sky clear, and prevent any clouds from forming for a while yet.

Anne Desbaresdes braved this weather, this wind, and reached the port after having passed the first breakwater and anchorage where the sand barges were moored, where the industrial section of the city began. She stopped again at the bar; the man was already

in the room waiting for her, no doubt still bound by
the ritual of the first meetings, which she instinctively
adhered to. She ordered some wine, still terribly
afraid. The patronne, who was behind the bar knitting her red wool, noticed they did not acknowledge
each other's presence for a long time after she had
come in, a sham that lasted longer than on the previous day. It lasted even after the child had joined his
new-found friend outside.

"I'd like another glass of wine," Anne Desbaresdes
said.

She was served with obvious disapproval. And yet,
when the man got up, went over to her, and took her
back into the semi-darkness of the back room, her
hands had already stopped shaking, the color had returned to her face.

"I'm not used to going so far away from home,"
she explained. "But it's not because I'm afraid. I
think it's more surprise, or something like it."

"It could be fear. People will get to know about
this in town, like they get to know everything," the
man added with a smile.

Outside the child shouted happily, because two tugboats were coming in side by side towards the anchorage. Anne Desbaresdes smiled.

"That I drink wine with you," she finished, suddenly exploding into a laugh. "Now why do I keep
wanting to laugh today?"

He moved his face close to hers, placed his hands against hers on the table, and stopped laughing when she stopped.

"The moon was almost full last night. You could see your garden very clearly, how well kept it is, smooth as glass. It was late. The light was still on in the hallway on the second floor."

"I told you, sometimes I have trouble sleeping."

He pretended to turn his glass in his hand to make things easier for her, put her at her ease, as he suspected she wanted him to, so she could look at him more closely. She looked at him more closely.

"I'd like a little wine," she said plaintively, as if she were hurt. "I didn't know you could acquire the habit so quickly. I've almost acquired it already."

He ordered the wine. They drank it together avidly, but this time nothing made Anne Desbaresdes drink except her nascent desire to become intoxicated from the wine. She drank, then paused, and in a soft, half-guilty voice began to question the man again.

"I'd like you to tell me now how they came not to speak to each other any more."

The child appeared in the doorway, saw that she was still there, and ran off again.

"I don't know. Perhaps through the long silences that grew up between them at night, then at other times, silences they found more and more difficult to overcome."

The same trouble that had closed Anne Desbaresdes' eyes the day before now made her hunch her shoulders forward dejectedly.

"One night they pace back and forth in their rooms, like caged animals, not knowing what's happening to them. They begin to suspect what it is, and are afraid."

"Nothing can satisfy them any longer."

"They're overwhelmed by what is happening, they can't talk about it yet. Perhaps it will take months. Months for them to know."

He paused for a moment before going on. He drank a full glass of wine. While he was drinking the sun was reflected in his eyes with all the exactitude of chance. She saw it.

"In front of a certain window on the first floor," he said, "there's a beech tree, one of the most beautiful trees in the garden."

"That's my room. It's a big room."

His mouth was moist from having drunk and, in the soft light, it too seemed implacably exact.

"They say it's a quiet room, the best room in the house."

"In summer this beech tree hides my view of the sea. One day I asked to have it removed, cut down. I must not have insisted enough."

He glanced above the bar to try to see what time it was.

"In a quarter of an hour work will be over, and very soon after that you'll be going home. We really have very little time. I don't think it matters one way or the other whether the beech tree is there or not. If I were you I'd let it go on growing, let its shadow grow a little every year on the walls of the room that is called—wrongly, I believe—yours."

She leaned way back in her chair, displaying her bust in a movement that was almost vulgar, and turned away from him.

"But sometimes its shadow is like black ink," she said softly.

"I don't think that matters."

He laughed as he handed her a glass of wine.

"That woman had become a drunkard. At night people found her in the bars out beyond the dock-yards, stone drunk. There was a lot of bad talk."

Anne Desbaresdes feigned astonishment, but over-did it.

"I suspected something, but nothing as bad as that. Maybe in their case it was necessary?"

"I don't know any more than you do. Talk to me."

"Yes." She dug deep. "Sometimes, on Saturday, one or two drunks also come along the Boulevard de la Mer singing at the top of their voices or making speeches. They go as far as the dunes, to the last lamp-post, and come back, still singing. Generally it's late when they come, when everyone else is asleep. I think they're brave to wander around in that section of town, it's so deserted."

"You're lying in bed in that big, quiet room, and you hear them. The room has a disorderly air about it that's not like you. You were lying there, you were."

Anne Desbaresdes stiffened and, as was sometimes her custom, went limp. Her voice deserted her. Her hands began to tremble slightly.

"They're going to extend the boulevard beyond the dunes," she said, "They're talking about doing it sometime soon."

"You were lying in bed. No one knew. In ten minutes it will be quitting time."

"I know it," said Anne Desbaresdes, "and . . . these last years at whatever time it was, I always knew, always . . . "

"Whether you were asleep or awake, dressed or naked, they passed outside the pale of your existence."

Anne Desbaresdes resisted, guilty, and yet she accepted it.

"You shouldn't," she said. "I remember, anything can happen . . . "

"Yes."

She kept staring at his mouth, which was the only thing still lighted by the dying rays of day.

"It would be easy to mistake that garden from a distance, since it's enclosed and overlooks the sea. Last

June—in a few days it will be a year ago—you were standing facing him on the steps, ready to receive us, the workers from the foundries. Above your breasts, which were half bare, there was a white magnolia. My name is Chauvin."

She resumed her usual position facing him, leaning on the table. Her face was already unsteady from the wine.

"I knew it. And I also knew that you left the foundries without reason and that you'll soon have to go back, because no other company in town has a job for you."

"Keep talking to me. Soon I won't ask you anything more."

Anne Desbaresdes began mechanically, like a schoolchild reciting a lesson she had never learned.

"When I came to this house the privet hedges were already there. When a storm approached they grated like steel. When you get used to it, it's like . . . like listening to your own heart. I got used to it. What you told me about that woman was a lie, about their finding her dead drunk in the bars by the dockyards."

The siren went off, right on time, deafening the whole town. The patronne checked the time and put her red sweater aside. Chauvin spoke as calmly as if he had not heard.

"Lots of women have already lived in that same house and listened to the hedges at night, in place of their hearts. The hedges have always been there. They all died in their room behind that beech tree which, by the way, you're wrong about: it has stopped growing."

"That's as much a lie as what you told me about their finding that woman dead drunk every night."

"Yes, that's a lie too. But this house is enormous. It covers hundreds of square yards. And it's so old that you can conjecture endlessly about it. It must be frightening."

She was seized by the same emotion, and closed her eyes. The patronne got up, moved around, began rinsing some glasses.

"Hurry up and say something. Make it up."

She made an effort; her voice was almost loud in the café, which was still empty.

"People ought to live in a town where there are no trees trees scream when there's a wind here there's always a wind always except for two days a year in your place don't you see I'd leave this place I wouldn't stay all the birds or almost all are seagulls you find them dead after a storm and when the storm is over the trees stop screaming you hear them screaming on the beach like someone murdered it keeps the children from sleeping no I'll leave."

She paused, her eyes still shut with fear. He looked at her attentively.

"Perhaps we're wrong," he said, "perhaps he wanted to kill her right away, the first time he saw her. Talk to me."

She couldn't. Her hands began to shake again, but for reasons other than fear and the turmoil that any allusion to her existence threw her into. So he talked instead, his voice calm again.

"It's true that it's so rare for the wind to stop in this town that when it does you feel stifled. I've already noticed it."

Anne Desbaresdes wasn't listening.

"Dead," she said, "even after she was dead she was still smiling happily."

The children's shouts and laughter exploded outside, greeting the evening as if it were dawn. From the south other shouts—of grown-ups, of men released from work—rose above the dull humming of the foundries.

"The wind never fails," Anne Desbaresdes went on wearily, "it always comes back and—I don't know whether you've ever noticed it—it varies from day to day. Sometimes it comes all of a sudden, especially at sundown, and sometimes very slowly, but then only when it's terribly hot, and in the wee hours of the morning, at dawn. The privet hedges shout, you know what I mean, that's how I know."

"You know everything about this one garden,

which is almost exactly like all the other gardens on the Boulevard de la Mer. In summer, when the privet hedges shout, you close your window to shut them out, and you're naked because of the heat."

"I'd like some wine," Anne Desbaresdes pleaded. "I keep wanting more wine . . . "

He ordered some wine.

"The siren went ten minutes ago," the patronne warned when she served them.

The first man arrived, and drank the same wine at the bar.

"In the left corner of the garden," Anne Desbaresdes went on in a near whisper, "there's an American copper beech to the north. I don't know why, I don't know at all why . . . "

The man at the bar recognized Chauvin, and nodded to him in a slightly embarrassed way. Chauvin didn't see him.

"Tell me more," Chauvin said, "you can tell me anything at all."

The child appeared, out of breath, his hair all mussed. The streets leading to the docks resounded with men's footsteps.

"Mother," the child said.

"In two minutes," Chauvin said, "she's leaving in two minutes."

The man at the bar tried to pat the child's head as he passed, but the boy broke away savagely.

"One day," Anne Desbaresdes said, "I had that child."

A dozen or so workers burst noisily into the café. Some of them recognized Chauvin. Again Chauvin didn't see them.

"Sometimes at night, when the child is sleeping," Anne Desbaresdes went on, "I go downstairs and walk in the garden. I go to the railings and look at the boulevard. It's very peaceful there at night, especially in winter. Sometimes in summer a few couples pass with their arms around each other, that's all. We picked that house because it's quiet, the quietest house in town. I must be going."

Chauvin leaned back in his chair, taking his time.

"You go to the railings, then you go away and walk around the house, then you come back again to the railings. The child is sleeping upstairs. You have never screamed. Never."

She put her suitcoat back on without replying. He helped her. She got up and once again remained standing beside him near the table, staring past the men at the bar. Some of them tried to make a sign of recognition to Chauvin, but to no avail. He was looking at the dock.

Anne Desbaresdes finally shook off her torpor.

"I'll be back," she said.

"Tomorrow."

He accompanied her to the door. Several groups

of men arrived, in a hurry. The child was in their wake. He ran to his mother, took her by the hand, and led her resolutely away. She followed him.

He told her that he had a new friend, and wasn't surprised that she didn't answer him. He stopped beside the empty beach—it was later than the day before—to watch the waves, which were rougher than usual that night. Then he started off again.

"Come on."

She let him lead, and started after him.

"You're walking slowly," he whined, "and it's cold."

"I can't go any faster."

She walked as fast as she could. The night, fatigue, and childhood made him cling to her, to his mother, and they walked on together. But since she was too drunk to see very far, she avoided looking towards the end of the boulevard, so as not to be discouraged by such a long distance.

"You'll remember now," Anne Desbaresdes said, "it means moderately and melodiously."

"Moderately and melodiously," the child repeated.

As they climbed the steps, the cranes rose in the sky to the south of town, turning with identical movements but at different speeds.

"I don't want her to scold you, I can't stand it."

"I don't want her to either. Moderately and melodiously."

A giant steam shovel, slobbering wet sand, swung into view through the last window on the floor, its teeth like those of a hungry beast gripping its prey.

"Music is necessary, and you have to learn it. Do you understand?"

"I understand."

Mademoiselle Giraud's apartment was high enough —it was on the sixth floor—so that its windows overlooked a wide expanse of ocean. Aside from the flight of the gulls, there was nothing to distract the child's attention.

"Well, did you learn what happened? A crime of passion. Please sit down, Madame Desbaresdes."

"What was it?" the child asked.

"All right now, quickly, the sonatina," Mademoiselle Giraud said.

The child sat down at the piano. Mademoiselle Giraud sat down beside him, the pencil in her hand. Anne Desbaresdes sat down on the other side of the room, near the window.

"The sonatina. Go ahead, Diabelli's pretty little sonatina. What is the tempo of this pretty little sonatina? Tell me."

The child cringed at the sound of her voice. He seemed to reflect, took his time, and perhaps lied.

"Moderately and melodiously," he said.

Mademoiselle Giraud crossed her arms, looked at him, and sighed.

"He does it deliberately. There's no other explanation."

The child did not bat an eyelash. His two little hands lay clenched on his knees, waiting for his torture to end, smug in the ineluctability of his own act, repeated over and over again.

70

"You can see the days are getting longer," Anne Desbaresdes said softly.

"They are indeed," said Mademoiselle Giraud.

The sun was noticeably higher in the sky than last week at the same time. And besides, it had been such a lovely day that the sky was covered with a haze, a light haze to be sure, but unusual for that time of year.

"I'm still waiting for your answer."

"Perhaps he didn't hear."

"He heard perfectly well. One thing you'll never understand, Madame Desbaresdes, is that he does it deliberately."

The child turned his head slightly towards the window, and looked obliquely at the watery mark on the wall made by the reflection of the sun on the sea. His mother was the only one who could see his eyes.

"Shame on you, darling," she whispered.

"In four-four time," the child said listlessly, without moving.

That evening his eyes were almost the same color as the sky, except that they sparkled with flecks of gold the color of his hair.

"Some day," his mother said, "some day he'll know it, and he'll say it without hesitating, it's inevitable. Even if he doesn't want to he'll know it."

She laughed gaily, silently.

"You ought to be ashamed, Madame Desbaresdes," said Mademoiselle Giraud.

"So they say."

She unfolded her arms, struck the keyboard with her pencil, just as she had been doing for the thirty years she had been teaching and shouted:

"Scales. Ten minutes of scales. To teach you a lesson. Begin with C major."

The child turned back to the piano, raised both hands and placed them on the keyboard with triumphant meekness.

A C major scale rose above the sound of the surf.

"Again. Again. That's the only way to teach boys like you."

The child began again at the point he had started the first time, the exact and mysterious point of the keyboard where it was necessary to start. A second, then a third C major scale rose amid Mademoiselle Giraud's anger.

"Again. I said ten minutes."

The child turned and looked at Mademoiselle Giraud, his hands resting quietly on the keyboard.

"Why?"

A look of such ugly rage filled Mademoiselle Giraud's face that the child turned back to the piano and froze in a pose of seemingly academic perfection. But he did not play.

"Really, he's impossible."

72

"They don't ask to come into this world," Anne Desbaresdes said with another laugh, "and then we force them to take piano lessons. What can you expect?"

Mademoiselle Giraud shrugged her shoulders, and without replying directly to Madame Desbaresdes, without replying to anyone in particular, composed herself and said for her own benefit:

"Strange how children end up by making you lose your temper."

"But one day he'll know his scales too,"—Anne Desbaresdes made an effort to placate her—"he'll know them as well as his tempo, I'm sure of it, he'll even be bored from knowing them so well."

"The way you bring that boy up is absolutely appalling, Madame," Mademoiselle Giraud shouted.

She seized the child's head with one hand and twisted it around, forcing him to look at her. He lowered his eyes.

"You'll play them because I told you to. And impertinent to boot. G major three times, if you please. And C major once more."

The child began playing the C major scale again. He played it a little more carelessly than the preceding times. Then he waited again.

"I said G major now. G major."

He dropped his hands from the keyboard. Stubbornly, he lowered his head. His little dangling feet,

73

still a long way from the pedals, rubbed angrily against each other.

"Perhaps you didn't hear what I said?"

"You heard," his mother said, "I'm sure you heard."

The child was seduced by the tenderness of the voice. Without answering, he again placed his hands on the keyboard at exactly the right spot. One, then two G major scales were encompassed by the mother's love. The siren from the dockyards signalled the end of the working day. The light was fading. The scales were so perfect the lady acknowledged them.

"It's good for the fingers as well as the character," she said.

"You're quite right," his mother said sadly.

But the child balked at playing the third G major scale.

"I said three times. Three."

This time the child withdrew his hands from the keyboard, placed them on his knees, and said:

"No."

The sun began to dip in such a way that suddenly, obliquely, the sea was illuminated. Mademoiselle Giraud grew utterly calm.

"The only thing I can say to you, Madame Desbaresdes, is that I pity you."

The child glanced surreptitiously at his mother, who was so much to be pitied and who was laughing. Then he sat rigidly at his post, his back necessarily to the sea. Twilight was falling, the rising wind crossed the room in little eddies, rustling the stubborn child's hair like grass. In silence his little feet began dancing jerkily under the piano.

"You don't mind playing it once more," his mother said laughingly, "just once more."

The child turned to her, ignoring his teacher.

"I don't like scales."

Mademoiselle Giraud watched both of them, first one then the other, not listening to what they were saying, too discouraged even to be indignant.

"I'm waiting."

The child turned back to the piano, but swung as far away as he could from the lady.

"Darling," his mother said, "just once more."

Her words made him blink. And yet he still hesitated.

"No scales then."

"Yes," she said, "you must play the scales."

He still hesitated, then, just as they were about to give up, he made up his mind and began to play. But Mademoiselle Giraud was too disturbed and frustrated to be placated.

"You know, Madame Desbaresdes, I don't know whether I can go on giving him lessons."

The G major scale was again perfect, perhaps faster than the time before, but only a trifle.

"I admit he's not really trying," his mother said.

When he had finished the scale the child, completely unperturbed by the passage of time, raised himself on the piano stool and tried to see what was going on below on the docks, but it was impossible.

"I'll explain to him that he'll have to apply himself," his mother said with false penitence.

Mademoiselle Giraud looked upset and said pompously:

"You shouldn't explain anything to him. It's not up to him to decide whether or not he's going to take piano lessons, Madame Desbaresdes. That's what is called education."

She struck the piano. The child gave up trying to see out the window.

"And now your sonatina. In four-four time."

The child played it as he had played the scales. He knew it perfectly. And although his heart was not in it, he played it musically, there was no denying.

"There's no getting around it," Mademoiselle Giraud went on above the music, "there are some children you have to be strict with. Or else they'll drive you to distraction."

"I'll try," Anne Desbaresdes said.

She listened to the sonatina. It came from the depths of the ages, borne to her by her son. Often, as she listened to it, she felt she was on the verge of fainting.

"The trouble is, don't you see, he thinks he can decide for himself he doesn't like to study the piano.

76

But I know perfectly well I'm wasting my breath saying that to you, Madame Desbaresdes."

"I'll try."

The sonatina still resounded, borne like a feather by this young barbarian, whether he liked it or not, and showered again on his mother, sentencing her anew to the damnation of her love. The gates of hell banged shut.

"Begin again, and this time play it a little more slowly."

The child did as she said, playing more slowly and subtly. Music flowed from his fingers as if, in spite of himself, it seemed to make up its mind, and artfully crept out into the world once again, overwhelming and engulfing the unknown heart. Down below, on the docks, they listened to it.

"He's been working on it for a month," the patronne said. "It's a pretty piece."

A first group of men was heading towards the café.

"Yes, at least a month," she added. "I know it by heart."

Chauvin, at the end of the bar, was still the only customer. He looked at the time, stretched and hummed the sonatina in time to the child's playing. The patronne kept an eye on him as she arranged the glasses under the counter.

"You're young," she said.

She estimated how long it would take the first group

of men to reach the café. She spoke quickly, but her words were well-meaning.

"Sometimes, you know, when the weather's good, I seem to remember that she goes the long way around, by the second dock. She doesn't always come this way."

"No," the man laughed.

The group of men passed the door.

"One, two, three, four," Mademoiselle Giraud counted, "that's the way."

Beneath the child's hands the sonatina flowed on, although he was unconscious of it—it built and re-built, borne by his indifferent clumsiness to the limits of its power. And as the music built, the light visibly declined. A huge peninsula of flaming clouds rose on the horizon, its frail and fleeting splendor compelling other thoughts. In ten minutes all the color of day would have vanished. For the third time the child finished his task. The sounds of the sea, mingled with the voices of the approaching men, rose to the room.

"By heart," said Mademoiselle Giraud. "Next time I want you to know it by heart, do you understand?"

"All right. By heart."

"I promise you he will," his mother said.

"Because it can't go on like this. He's making fun of me. It's outrageous."

"I promise."

Mademoiselle Giraud reflected, not listening.

"We might try having someone else come with him to his lessons," she said. "We could see if it did any good."

"No," the child shouted.

"I don't think I could bear that," Anne Desbaresdes said.

"And yet I'm afraid that's what it will have to come to," said Mademoiselle Giraud.

When the door was closed, the child stopped on the staircase.

"You saw how awful she was."

"Do you do it deliberately?"

The child gazed at the cluster of cranes, now motionless in the sky. The lights in the suburbs were coming on.

"I don't know," the child said.

"I love you so much."

The child began slowly descending the stairs.

"I don't want to take any more piano lessons."

"I never could learn the scales," Anne Desbaresdes said, "but how else can you learn?"

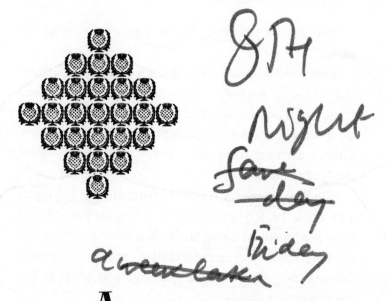

Anne Desbaresdes did not go in, but
paused at the door of the café. Chauvin came over to
her. When he reached her she turned towards the
Boulevard da la Mer.

"There are so many people here now," she said
softly. "These piano lessons finish so late."

"I heard the lesson," Chauvin said.

The child let go of her hand and fled to the sidewalk, wanting to run, as he ran every Friday evening
at that time. Chauvin raised his head towards the dark
blue sky, which was still faintly lighted, and moved
closer to her. She did not move back.

"It'll soon be summer," he said. "Come on."

"But here you can hardly tell the difference."

"Sometimes you can. If you know how. Like to-night."

The child jumped over the rope barriers, singing the Diabelli sonatina. Anne Desbaresdes followed Chauvin. The café was full. The men dutifully drank their wine as soon as it was served, and hurried home. Others, arriving from more distant factories, replaced them at the bar.

When she entered Anne Desbaresdes lost her nerve and drew back near the door. Chauvin turned and gave her an encouraging smile. She went to the end of the bar, which was fairly secluded, and, like the men, downed her glass of wine quickly. The glass in her hand was still shaking.

"It's been seven days now," Chauvin said.

"Seven nights," Anne said casually. "How wonderful wine is."

They left the bar, and he took her to the back of the room and had her sit down at the place he had picked out for her. The men at the bar still looked at this woman, but distantly, and were still surprised. The room was quiet.

"So you heard the lesson? And all those scales she made him play?"

"It was early. I was the only customer. The windows overlooking the docks must have been open. I heard everything, even the scales."

She smiled gratefully at him, and drank some more.

Her hands, holding the glass, were almost calm now.

"I somehow got the idea that he had to learn music, you know. He's been studying for two years."

"Sure, I understand. So, this grand piano, to the left as you go into the room?"

"Yes." Anne Desbaresdes clenched her fists and struggled to maintain her composure. "But he's still so little, such a little child, you have no idea. When I think about it, I wonder whether I'm not wrong."

Chauvin laughed. They were still the only ones seated at the back of the room. There were fewer customers at the bar now.

"Do you know that he knows his scales perfectly?"

Anne Desbaresdes laughed, this time wholeheartedly.

"Yes, he knows them. Even his teacher had to admit that, you see . . . sometimes I get strange ideas . . . They make me laugh to think of them now."

As her laughter began to subside Chauvin spoke to her in a different way.

"You were leaning on this grand piano. Your breasts were naked under your dress, and between them there was that magnolia flower."

Anne Desbaresdes listened to his story with rapt attention.

"Yes."

"When you lean forward this flower brushes against the outline of your breasts. You'd pinned it carelessly, too high up. It's a huge flower, too big for you, you picked it at random. Its petals are too hard, it has already reached full bloom the night before."

"I'm looking outside?"

"Have a little more wine. The child is playing in the garden. Yes, you're looking outside."

Anne Desbaresdes did as she was asked, and drank some more wine, trying to remember, then returned from the depths of her surprise.

"I can't remember having picked that flower. Or having worn it."

"I only glanced at you, but long enough to see the flower too."

She concentrated on holding the glass very tightly, and her voice and gestures seemed slow and wooden.

"I never really knew how much I liked wine."

"Now, talk to me."

"Oh, let me alone," Anne Desbaresdes begged.

"I can't, we probably have so little time."

Twilight was so far advanced that only the café ceiling reflected the last pale light of day. The bar was brightly lighted, the room in shadow. The child came running up, not surprised at how late it was, and announced:

"The other little boy's arrived."

In the moment following his departure, Chauvin's

hands moved closer to hers. All four lay flat on the table.

"As I told you, sometimes I have trouble sleeping. I go into his room and stand there looking at him."

"And other times?"

"And other times it's summer, and there are people strolling along the boulevard. Especially on Saturday evening, no doubt because people don't know what to do with themselves in this town."

"No doubt," Chauvin said. "Especially the men. You often watch them from that hallway, or from your garden, or from your room."

Anne Desbaresdes leaned forward and finally said to him:

"Yes, I think I often must have watched them, either from the hallway or from my room, on nights when I didn't know what to do with myself."

Chauvin murmured something to her. Her expression slowly dissolved at the insult, and softened.

"Go on."

"Apart from these walks, the day has a fixed routine. I can't go on."

"There's very little time left. Go on."

"There's the endless round of meals. And the evenings. One day I got the idea of these piano lessons."

They finished their wine. Chauvin ordered another. There were even fewer men at the bar now. Anne

Desbaresdes drank again as if she were terribly thirsty.

"It's already seven o'clock," the patronne warned.

They didn't hear her. It was dark out. Four men, obviously there to kill time, came to the back room. The radio was announcing the weather for the following day.

"I was saying that I had the idea of these piano lessons for my darling—at the other end of town—and now I can't do without them. It's seven o'clock, you know."

"You're going to arrive home later than usual, maybe too late, you can't avoid it. You'd better resign yourself to the idea."

"How can you avoid a fixed routine? I could tell you that I'm already late for dinner, counting the time it will take me to walk home. And besides, I forgot that I'm supposed to be home for a party tonight."

"You know that there's no way you can avoid arriving home late. You know that, don't you?"

"Yes, I know it."

He waited. She spoke to him in a quiet, offhand manner.

"I could tell you that I told my child about all those women who lived behind that beech tree, and are dead now, and he wanted to know if he could see them, the darling. See, I've just told you all I can tell you."

"As soon as you'd told him about the women you were sorry you had, and you told him about the vacation he's going to spend this year—a few days from now—at another seashore?"

"I promised him a vacation at the seashore, somewhere where it's hot. In two weeks time. He was terribly upset about the death of those women."

Anne Desbaresdes drank some more wine, and found it strong. She smiled, but her eyes were glassy.

"It's getting late. And you're making yourself later and later," Chauvin said.

"When being late becomes as serious a matter as it is now for me," Anne Desbaresdes said, "I think that a little while longer isn't going to make it any more serious."

There was only one customer left at the bar. The four others in the room were talking intermittently. A couple came in. The patronne served them, and resumed knitting her red sweater, which she had put aside as long as the bar was crowded. She turned down the radio. The tide was running high that night, breaking loudly against the docks, rising above the songs.

"Once he had realized how much she wanted him to do it, I'd like you to tell me why he didn't do it, say, a little later or . . . a little sooner."

"Really, I know very little about it. But I think that he couldn't make up his mind, couldn't decide whether he wanted her alive or dead. He must have decided very late in the game that he preferred her dead. But that's all pure conjecture."

Anne Desbaresdes was lost in thought, her pale face lowered hypocritically.

"She hoped very much that he would do it."

"It seems to me that he must have hoped so just as much as she did. I don't know really."

"As much as she did?"

"Yes. Don't talk any more."

The four men left. The couple was still sitting there in silence. The woman yawned. Chauvin ordered another bottle of wine.

"Would it be impossible if we didn't drink so much?"

"I don't think it would be possible," Anne Desbaresdes murmured.

She gulped down her glass of wine. He let her go on killing herself. Night had completely occupied the town. The lampposts along the docks were lighted. The child was still playing. The last trace of pink had faded from the sky.

"Before I leave," Anne Desbaresdes begged, "if you could tell me I'd like to know a little more. Even if you're not very sure of your facts."

Chauvin went on, in a flat, expressionless voice that she had not heard from him before.

"They lived in an isolated house, I think it was by the sea. It was hot. Before they went there they didn't realize how quickly things would evolve, that after a few days he would keep having to throw her out. It wasn't long before he was forced to drive her away, away from him, from the house. Over and over again."

"It wasn't worth the trouble."

"It must have been difficult to keep from having such thoughts, you get into the habit, like you get into the habit of living. But it's only a habit."

"And she left?"

"She left when and how he wanted her to, although she wanted to stay."

Anne Desbaresdes stared at that unknown man without recognizing him, like a trapped animal.

"Please," she begged.

"Then the time came when he sometimes looked at her and no longer saw her as he had seen her before. She ceased to be beautiful or ugly, young or old, similar to anyone else, even to herself. He was afraid. It was the last vacation. Winter came. You're going back by the Boulevard de la Mer. It will be the eighth night."

The child came in and snuggled for a moment against his mother. He was still humming the Diabelli sonatina. She stroked his hair, which was very close to her face. The man avoided looking at them. Then the child left.

"So the house was isolated," Anne Desbaresdes

said slowly. "It was hot, you said. When he told her to leave she always obeyed. She slept under the trees, or in the fields, like . . . "

"Yes," Chauvin said.

"When he called her she came back. And when he told her to go, she left. To obey him like that was her way of hoping. And even when she reached the threshold she waited for him to tell her to come in."

"Yes."

In a daze, Anne Desbaresdes brought her face close to Chauvin's, but he moved back out of reach.

"And it was there, in that house, that she learned what you said she was, perhaps even . . . "

"Yes, a bitch," Chauvin interrupted her again.

Now it was her turn to draw back. He filled her glass and offered it to her.

"I was lying," he said.

She arranged her hair, which was completely disheveled, and wearily trying to restrain her compassion, got hold of herself.

"No," she said.

Chauvin's face looked inhumanly harsh under the neon light, but she could not take her eyes off him. Again the child ran in from the sidewalk.

"It's dark out now," he announced.

He looked out the door and yawned, then turned back to her and stood beside her, humming.

"See how late it is. Quickly, tell me the rest."

"Then the time came when he thought he could no longer touch her except to . . ."

Anne Desbaresdes raised her hands to her bare neck in the opening of her summer dress.

"Except to . . . this. Am I right?"

"Yes. That."

Her hands let go and slipped from her neck.

"I'd like you to leave," Chauvin murmured.

Anne Desbaresdes got up from her chair and stood motionless in the middle of the room. Chauvin remained seated, overwhelmed, no longer aware of her. Unable to resist, the patronne put her knitting aside, and openly watched them both, but they were oblivious of her stare. It was the child who came to the door and took his mother's hand.

"Come on, let's go."

The lights were already on along the Boulevard de la Mer. It was much later than usual, an hour later at least. The child sang the sonatina one last time, then grew tired of it. The streets were almost deserted. People were already eating supper. After they had passed the first breakwater, the Boulevard de la Mer stretched endlessly before them. Anne Desbaresdes stopped.

"I'm too tired," she said.

"But I'm hungry," the child whined.

He saw that his mother's eyes were filled with tears. His whimpering ceased.

"Why are you crying?"

"For no reason. Sometimes people just cry."

"Please don't."

"It's all over, darling. I think it's all over."

He forgot and ran on ahead, then retraced his steps, revelling in this unaccustomed freedom after dark.

"At night," he said, "the houses are far away."

SEVEN

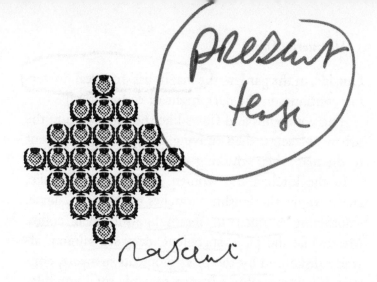

present tense

nascent

The salmon, chilled in its original form, is served on a silver platter that the wealth of three generations has helped to buy. Dressed in black, and with white gloves, a man carries it like a royal child, and offers it to each guest in the silence of the nascent dinner. It is proper not to talk about it.

At the northern end of the garden the scent of magnolias arises, drifting from dune to dune till it disappears. Tonight the wind is from the south. A man prowls along the Boulevard de la Mer. A woman knows he is there.

The salmon passes from guest to guest, following a ritual that nothing can disturb, except everyone's hidden fear that such perfection may suddenly be marred or sullied by some excessively obvious absurdity.

Outside, in the garden, the magnolias' funereal flowering continues in the dark night of early spring.

The wind ebbs and flows like the surf, striking the urban obstacles, then moving on, wafting the scent to the man, then whisking it away again.

In the kitchen the women, their honor at stake, sweat to put the finishing touches to the next course, smothering a duck in its orange-shrouded coffin. Meanwhile the pink, succulent, deep-sea salmon, already disfigured by the brief moments just past, continues its ineluctable advance towards total annihilation, slowly dispelling the fear of an unsuccessful evening.

A man, facing a woman, looks at her as though he does not recognize her. Her breasts are again half exposed. She hastily adjusts her dress. A drooping flower lies between them. There are still flashes of lucidity in her wildly protruding eyes, enough for her to succeed in helping herself to some of their salmon when it comes her turn.

In the kitchen, now that the duck is ready and put into the oven to keep warm, they finally find a moment of peace to put their thoughts to words, saying that she is really going a bit too far. Tonight she arrived later than the night before, well after her guests had arrived.

Fifteen people had waited for her in the main living room on the ground floor. She had entered that glittering assembly without so much as the slightest apology. Someone apologized for her.

"Anne is late. Please forgive Anne."

For ten years she has never been the subject of any gossip. If she is bothered by her incongruity, she is unaware of it. A fixed smile makes her face acceptable.

"Anne didn't hear what you said."

She puts her fork down, looks around, tries to grasp the thread of conversation, fails.

"That's true," she says.

They ask again. Her blond hair is mussed, and she runs her fingers listlessly through it, as she had done a little while before in a different setting. Her lips are pale. Tonight she forgot to make herself up.

"I'm sorry," she says, "right now a sonatina by Diabelli."

"A sonatina? Already?"

"That's right."

Silence moves in again around the question, and the fixed smile returns to her face. She is a wild animal.

"He didn't know what moderato cantabile meant?"

"No, he didn't."

Tonight the magnolias will be in full bloom. Except for the one she is wearing, the one she picked tonight on her way home from the port. Time moves monotonously past this forgotten flowering.

"Darling, how could he have guessed?"

"He couldn't."

"He's sleeping, I suppose."

"Yes, he's sleeping."

Slowly the digestion of what was a salmon begins. The osmosis of the species that ate it was carried out like a perfect ritual. Nothing upset the solemnity of the process. The other waits, snug and warm, in its orange shroud. And now the moon rises on the sea, and on the man lying on the ground. Through the white curtains you now could barely distinguish the shapes and forms of night. Madame Desbaresdes contributes nothing to the conversation.

"Mademoiselle Giraud told me that story yesterday. She gives my little boy lessons also, you know."

"Is that so?"

People laugh. A woman somewhere around the table. Little by little the chorus of conversation grows louder and, with considerable effort and ingenuity, some sort of society emerges. Landmarks are discovered, cracks open, allowing familiarities to slip in. And little by little a generally biased and individually noncommittal conversation builds up. It will be a successful party. The women bask in their own brilliance. The men have covered them with jewels according to their bankrolls. Tonight one of them suspects he may have made a mistake.

In the sequestered garden the birds sleep peacefully, for the weather is still fine. The same sort of sleep as the child's. The remains of the salmon are offered around again. The women will devour it to the last mouthful. Their bare shoulders have the gloss and solidity of a society founded and built on the certainty of its rights, and they were chosen to fit this society. Their strict education has taught them that they must temper their excesses in the interest of their position. They stuff themselves with mayonnaise, specially prepared for this dish, forget themselves, and lap it up. The men look at them and remember that therein lies their happiness.

Tonight one of them does not share the others' appetite. She comes from the other end of town, from beyond the breakwaters and oil depots at the other end of the Boulevard de la Mer, from beyond the limits imposed upon her ten years before, where a man had offered her more wine than she could handle. Full of this wine, an exception to the general rule, she could not bring herself to eat. Beyond the white blinds lay darkness, and in this darkness a man, with plenty of time to kill, stands looking now at the sea, now at the garden. Then at the sea, at the garden, at his hands. He doesn't eat. He cannot eat either, his body obsessed by another hunger. The capricious wind still bears the scent of magnolias to him, taking him by surprise, tormenting him as much as the scent of a single flower. A light in the second story was turned out a little while ago, and was not turned back on. They must have closed the windows on that side of the house, to shut out the oppressive odor of the flowers at night.

Anne Desbaresdes keeps on drinking. Tonight the champagne has the annihilating taste of the unknown lips of the man outside in the street.

The man has left the Boulevard de la Mer and circled the garden, keeping watch from the dunes which bound it on the north, then he has retraced his steps and descended the slope to the beach. And there he lay down again in the same place. He stretches, stares for a moment out to sea, then turns and looks again at the bay windows with their white blinds. Then he gets up, picks up a pebble, aims at the windows, turns back again, tosses the pebble into the sea, lies down, stretches again, and says a name out loud.

Two women, alternately and cooperatively, prepare the second course. The other victim is waiting.

"As you know, Anne is defenseless when it comes to her child."

Her smile broadens. The remark is repeated. Again she runs her fingers through the blond disorder of her hair. The circles under her eyes are deeper than before. Tonight she cried. By now the moon has risen above the town, and above the man lying on the beach.

"That's true," she says.

alienation

Her hand falls from her hair, and pauses at the wilting magnolia at her breast.

"We're all alike really."

"Yes," Anne Desbaresdes says.

The petals of the magnolia are smooth. Her fingers crumple it, pierce the petals, then stop, paralyzed, lie on the table, wait, affecting an attitude of nonchalance, but in vain. For someone has noticed it. Anne Desbaresdes tries to smile apologetically, as if to imply that she couldn't help it, but she is drunk, and her expression shamelessly betrays it. He scowls, but remains impassive. He has already recovered from his surprise. He has alway expected as much.

With half-closed eyes, Anne Desbaresdes drinks another glass of wine in one swallow. She has reached the point where she can't help it. She derives from drink a confirmation of what was till then her hidden desire, and a base consolation for that discovery.

Other women drink in turn, raising their bare arms, their enticing, irreproachable, matronly arms. The man on the beach is whistling a tune heard that afternoon in a café at the port.

The moon has risen, and as the night advances it begins to grow cold. Perhaps the man is cold.

They begin to serve the pressed duck. The women help themselves generously, fully capable of doing justice to the delicacy. They murmur softly in admiration as the golden duck is passed around. The

her husband

sight of it makes one of them grow faint. Her mouth
is desiccated by another hunger that nothing, except
perhaps the wine, can satisfy. A song she cannot sing
comes back to her, a song heard that afternoon in a
café at the port. The man is still alone on the beach.

He has just spoken the name again, and his mouth
is still half open.

"No thank you."

The man's closed eyes are caressed by the wind,
and, in powerful, impalpable waves, by the scent of
the magnolias, as the wind ebbs and flows.

Anne Desbaresdes has just declined to take any of
the duck. And yet the platter is still there before her,
only for a brief moment, but long enough for everyone to notice. She raises her hand, as she has been
taught to do, to emphasize her refusal. The platter is
removed. Silence settles around the table.

"I just couldn't. I'm sorry."

Again she raises her hand to her breast, to the
dying flower whose scent slips beyond the garden
and drifts to the sea.

"Perhaps it's that flower," someone suggests, "the
scent is so strong."

"No, I'm used to it. It's nothing really."

The duck continues on its course. Someone op-
posite her looks on impassively. And again she tries to
force a smile, but succeeds only in twisting her face

into a desperate, licentious grimace of confession. Anne Desbaresdes is drunk.

Again she is asked if she is not ill. She is not ill.

"Perhaps that flower," the voice insists, "is making you nauseous without your knowing it."

"No, I'm used to the scent of magnolias. I just don't happen to be hungry."

They leave her alone, and begin to devour the duck. Its flesh will be digested in other bodies. A man in the street closes his eyes, his eyelids fluttering from such willful patience. His body is chilled to the bone, and nothing can warm him. Again his mouth has uttered a name.

In the kitchen they announce that she has refused the pressed duck, that she is ill, there is no other explanation for it. Here they are talking of other things. The meaningless shapes of the magnolias caress the eyes of the solitary man. Once again Anne Desbaresdes takes her glass, which has just been refilled, and drinks. Unlike the others, its warmth fires her witch's loins. Her breasts, heavy on either side of the heavy flower, suffer from its sudden collapse, and hurt her. Her mouth, filled with wine, encompasses a name she does not speak. All this is accomplished in painful silence.

The man has left the beach and approached the garden railings. He seizes them and grips them tightly.

The lights are still on in the bay windows. How come it has not yet happened?

The pressed duck is passed around again. With the same gesture as before Anne Desbaresdes implores him not to serve her. She is passed by. She returns to the silent agony of her loins, to their burning pain, to her lair.

The man has let go of the garden railings. He looks at his empty hands, distorted by the strain. There, at arm's length, a destiny was decided.

The sea wind blows cooler through the town. Most people are already asleep. The second story windows are dark and closed, to keep the scent of the magnolias from disturbing the child's sleep. Red motorboats sail through his innocent dreams.

Some of the guests have taken a second helping of duck. The conversation flows more and more easily, increasing the distance of the night with every passing minute.

Bathed in the brilliant light of the chandeliers, Anne Desbaresdes continues to smile and say nothing.

The man has decided to leave the garden and walk to the edge of town. As he goes, the scent of the magnolias grows fainter, giving way to the smell of the sea.

Anne Desbaresdes will accept a little coffee ice cream, for the sake of appearances.

In spite of himself the man will retrace his steps.

Again he sees the magnolias, the railings, the bay windows in the distance, still lighted, still lighted. On his lips, the song heard that afternoon, and the name that he will utter a little louder this time. He will come.

She knows it. The magnolia at her breast is completely wilted. In one hour it has lived through a whole summer. Sooner or later the man will pass by the garden. He has come. She keeps torturing the flower at her breast.

"Anne didn't hear what you said."

She tries to smile more broadly, but it is useless. The words are repeated. One last time she runs her fingers through her blond hair. The circles under her eyes are even darker than before. Tonight she cried. They repeat the words for her benefit alone, and wait.

"Yes," she says, "we're going on vacation. We're taking a house by the sea. It will be hot there. In a house off by itself at the seashore."

"Darling," someone says.

"Yes."

While the guests pass from the dining room into the main living room, Anne Desbaresdes will go upstairs. From the big bay window of the long corridor of her life she will look at the boulevard below. The man will already have left. She will go into the child's room, and lie down on the floor at the foot of the bed, paying no attention to the magnolia crushed to pieces between her breasts. And to the inviolable rhythm of her child's breathing she will vomit forth the strange nourishment that had been forced upon her.

A shadow will appear in the doorway leading into the hall, deepening the shadow of the room. Anne Desbaresdes will run her hand through her disheveled hair. This time she will offer an apology.

The shadow will not reply.

the *hidden*

EIGHT

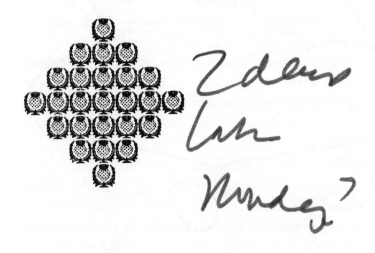

The good weather continued. It had lasted longer than anyone had dared hope. People talked about it now with a smile, as of a completely unseasonal phenomenon whose very persistence concealed some irregularity that would soon be discovered, thus reassuring everyone that the seasons were indeed following their normal course.

Today, even compared to the previous days, the weather was so lovely, at least for that time of year, that when the sky was not too overcast, when the sun shone through for a while, it would have been easy to believe that the weather was better, more precocious, more summery, than ever. In fact it took so long for the clouds to cover the sun that today was almost more beautiful than the preceding days had

(handwritten: What is the relevance of this?)

been. Even the seawind was balmy, much like the wind of certain summer days still far away.

Some people declared that the day had been hot. Others—and they were the majority—did not deny it had been a beautiful day, but claimed that it had nevertheless not been hot. Still others had no opinion.

Anne Desbaresdes did not return to the port till the second day following her previous visit. She arrived only slightly later than usual. As soon as Chauvin saw her—she was still a good distance away, beyond the breakwater—he went back into the café to wait for her. The child was not with her.

Anne Desbaresdes entered the café during one of those moments when the sun was out from behind the clouds for a long time. The patronne, seated in the shadow behind the counter, did not lift her eyes from her knitting when she came in. The knitting was progressing nicely. Anne Desbaresdes joined Chauvin at their usual table in the back of the room. Chauvin had not shaved that morning, but only the day before. Anne Desbaresdes' face was not as carefully made up as usual. Neither of them seemed to notice it.

"You're alone," Chauvin said.

It took her a long time to acknowledge that obvious fact. She tried to evade it, and was again surprised to find she could not.

"Yes."

To escape the stifling simplicity of this confession she turned towards the café door, towards the sea. To the south the foundries were humming. There, in the port, the sand and coal were being unloaded as usual.

"It's a nice day," she said.

Chauvin followed her gaze and looked outside, squinting at the weather, at what kind of weather it was out today.

"I wouldn't have believed it could happen so quickly."

In the ensuing silence the patronne turned around and switched on the radio, with no show of impatience, rather almost tenderly. In a foreign town, a woman sang. It was Anne Desbaresdes who moved closer to Chauvin.

"Starting this week someone else is taking my child to Mademoiselle Giraud for his lesson. I finally agreed that someone else should take him."

She sipped her wine, till she had emptied her glass. Chauvin forgot to order more.

"That's no doubt a better arrangement."

A customer came in, obviously to kill time, obviously lonely, very lonely, and also ordered some wine. The patronne served him, then went over and served the others in the room, without waiting to be asked.

They said nothing to her, but immediately began to drink the wine. Anne Desbaresdes' words came out in a rush.

"I threw up the wine I drank last time," she said. "It was only a few days ago I started drinking . . ."

"It doesn't matter now."

"Please . . . " she begged.

"I suppose we'd really better decide whether to talk or say nothing. Whichever you like."

She looked around the café, then at him, then around again, then at him, looking for help that was not forthcoming.

"I've been sick before, but never from drinking. For very different reasons. I was never used to drinking so much wine at once. I mean in such a short time. It made me sick. I couldn't stop. I thought I would never be able to stop. But then all of a sudden I had to stop, however hard I tried not to. It wasn't any longer a question of wanting or not wanting to."

Chauvin put his elbow on the table and held his head in his hands.

"I'm tired."

Anne Desbaresdes filled her glass and passed it to him. He didn't refuse.

"I can keep quiet," she said apologetically.

"No."

He laid his hand beside hers on the table, in the shadow cast by his body.

"The garden gate was locked as usual. The weather was lovely, almost no wind. The bay windows on the ground floor were lighted."

The patronne put her red sweater aside, rinsed some glasses, and, for the first time, did not seem concerned about whether they would stay on for a while or not. It was close to quitting time.

"We don't have much time left," Chauvin said.

The sun began to set. He watched it draw slow, fawn-colored patterns on the back wall.

"My child," Anne Desbaresdes said, "I didn't have time to tell you . . ."

"I know," Chauvin said.

She withdrew her hand from the table, and kept staring at Chauvin's hand which was still there. It was shaking. Then, in her impatience, she moaned softly—so softly that the sound of the radio covered it, and he alone heard it.

"Sometimes," she said, "I think I must have invented him."

"I know all I want to about your child," Chauvin said harshly.

Anne Desbaresdes moaned again, louder than before. Again she put her hand on the table. His eyes followed her movement and finally, painfully, he understood and lifted his own leaden hand and placed it on hers. Their hands were so cold they were touching only in intention, an illusion, in order for this

What does this mean?

to be fulfilled, for the sole reason that it should be fulfilled, none other, it was no longer possible. And yet, with their hands frozen in this funereal pose, Anne Desbaresdes stopped moaning.

"One last time," she begged, "tell me about it one last time."

Chauvin hesitated, his eyes somewhere else, still fixed on the back wall. Then he decided to tell her about it as if it were a memory.

"He had never dreamed, before meeting her, that he would one day want anything so badly."

"And she acquiesced completely?"

"Wonderfully."

Anne Desbaresdes looked at Chauvin absently. Her voice became thin, almost childlike.

"I'd like to understand why his desire to have it happen one day was so wonderful?"

Chauvin still avoided looking at her. Her voice was steady, wooden, the voice of a deaf person.

"There's no use trying to understand. It's beyond understanding."

"You mean there are some things like that that can't be gone into?"

"I think so."

Anne Desbaresdes' expression became dull, almost stupid. Her lips had turned pale, they were gray and trembled as though she were on the verge of tears.

"She does nothing to try and stop him?" she whispered.

"No. Have a little more wine."

She sipped her wine. He also drank, and his lips on the glass were also trembling.

"Time," he said.

"Does it take a long time, a very long time?"

"Yes, a very long time. But I don't know anything." He lowered his voice. "Like you, I don't know anything. Nothing at all."

Anne Desbaresdes' forced back her tears. Her voice was normal, momentarily awake.

"She will never speak again," she said.

"Of course she will. Suddenly one day, one beautiful morning, she'll meet someone she knows and won't be able to avoid saying good morning. Or she'll hear a child singing, it will be a lovely day and she'll remark how lovely it is. It will begin again."

"No."

"You can think whatever you like about it, it doesn't matter."

The siren went off, a loud wail that quickly spread to the far corners of the town and even beyond, into the suburbs, and to certain neighboring villages, borne by the sea wind. The sunset was a welter of even brighter yellow on the far wall. As often at sunset, the clouds billowed in fat clusters in the still sky, revealing the last fiery rays of the sun. That evening it seemed that the siren would never stop. But it finally did.

"I'm afraid," Anne Desbaresdes murmured.

Chauvin moved closer to the table, searched for her, searching for her, then gave up.

"I can't."

Then she did what he had been unable to do. She moved close enough to him for their lips to meet. They lingered in a long embrace, their lips cold and trembling, so that it should be accomplished, performing the same mortuary ritual as their hands had performed a moment before. It was accomplished.

From the nearby streets a subdued murmur reached them, punctuated by calm, carefree shouts. The dockyards nearby had opened their gates to eight hundred men. The patronne turned on the neon light above the bar, although the place was flooded with sun. After a moment's hesitation she went over to the now silent couple and solicitously served them some wine, although they had not asked for it. Then she remained there after she had served them, close to their table, hunting for something to say, but she found nothing and moved away.

"I'm afraid," Anne Desbaresdes said again.

Chauvin did not reply.

"I'm afraid," Anne Desbaresdes almost shouted.

Still Chauvin did not reply. Anne Desbaresdes

doubled over, her forehead almost touching the table, and accepted her fear.

"So we're going to leave things just as they are," Chauvin said. "That happens sometimes," he added.

A group of workers, who had already seen them there before, entered the café. Like the patronne and everyone else in town, they knew what was going on, and avoided looking at them. The café resounded with the chorus of various conversations.

Anne Desbaresdes raised her head, and tried to reach Chauvin across the table.

"Maybe I won't be able to," she murmured.

Perhaps he wasn't listening any longer. She pulled her suitcoat tightly around her, and buttoned it. Again she moaned, and was surprised to hear herself.

"That's impossible," she said.

Chauvin heard that.

"Wait a minute," he said, "and we'll be able to."

Anne Desbaresdes waited a minute, then she tried to stand up. She succeeded in getting to her feet. Chauvin was not looking at her. The men still kept their eyes turned away from this adulteress. She stood there.

"I wish you were dead," Chauvin said.

"I am." Anne Desbaresdes said.

Anne Desbaresdes moved around her chair so as to avoid having to sit down again. Then she took one step back and turned around. Chauvin's hand fluttered and fell to the table. But she was already too far away to see him.

She passed the cluster of men at the bar and found herself again moving forward into the fiery red rays of the dying day.

After she had left, the patronne turned the radio up louder. Some of the men complained that in their opinion it was too loud.

By the same author

NOVELS
  The Square
  The Afternoon of Monsieur Andesmas
  The Sailor from Gibraltar
  The Little Horses of Tarquinia
  Moderato Cantabile
  Ten-Thirty on a Summer Night
  The Duras Trilogy (The Square, Ten-Thirty on a Summer
    Night, The Afternoon of Monsieur Andesmas)

SHORT STORIES
  Whole Days in the Trees

PLAYS
  Three Plays (Days in the Trees, The Square, The Viaducts of
    Seine-et-Oise)
  The River and the Forest (*contained in* The Afternoon of
    Monsieur Andesmas)
  Suzanna Andler (*also* La Musica *and* L'Amante Anglaise)

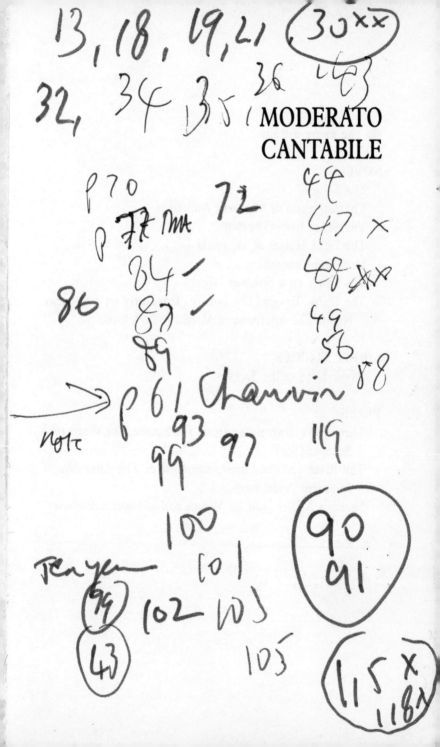